TWO CAN
TOUCAN

TWO CAN TOUCAN

David McKee

Andersen Press·London

For Chantel and Chuck

Text © 1964 by David McKee. Illustrations © 1985 by David McKee.

This paperback edition first published in 2001 by Andersen Press Ltd.

The rights of David McKee to be identified as the author and illustrator of this work have been asserted

by him in accordance with the Copyright, Designs and Patents Act, 1988.

First published in Great Britain in 1985 by Andersen Press Ltd., 20 Vauxhall Bridge Road, London SW1V 2SA.

Published in Australia by Random House Australia Pty., Level 3, 100 Pacific Highway, North Sydney, NSW 2060.

All rights reserved.

Colour separated in Switzerland by Photolitho AG, Zürich.

Printed and bound in Italy by Grafiche AZ, Verona.

10   9   8   7   6

British Library Cataloguing in Publication Data available.

ISBN 978 184270 0365

This book has been printed on acid-free paper

There was once a bird who didn't have a name. He had a very large beak and was all black except for the whites of his eyes.

All the other creatures, who had names, laughed at him. This made him very unhappy.

One day he decided to leave them all and go to seek his fortune.

He went over the mountain . . .

Then across the river . . .

Until he came to a hot dusty place where everybody worked.
This made him want to work as well.

So he went to see a man, sitting behind a large desk, who told him what to try.

At first he tried chopping wood, but his beak was so large that it always got in the way.

Next he tried office work, but he felt silly in a bowler hat.

Finally he tried carrying things. He enjoyed doing this and was very good at it.

Most of the time he carried cans. Because of his long beak
he could carry two at once.

The others called him "Two Can" as they could only carry one. He was happy, at last he had a name.

One day when Two Can was carrying paint, instead of being content with two he tried to carry three cans.

Going down some steps, he fell and ended up with orange, red and white paint all over him.

Although he scrubbed and scrubbed, he could not get the paint off.

He felt he was a failure, and one morning, before the city was awake, he left for home.

He went back across the river . . .

Then back over the mountain . . .

When at last he arrived home none of the creatures
recognized him in his fine new feathers.

When they asked his name, he said it was "Two Can".

They spelled it T-O-U-C-A-N so he decided to keep it that way.

Toucan explained who he was and told them about his adventures. When they heard the story they all laughed again.

But this time Toucan laughed with them!

Other Andersen Press picture books by
DAVID MCKEE:

Charlotte's Piggy Bank

Isabel's Noisy Tummy

Mr Benn, Gladiator

Not Now, Bernard!

The Conquerors

Three Monsters

Tusk Tusk